Bruno in the Snow

Written and Illustrated by
Sylvie Daigneault

HarperCollinsPublishersLtd

Produced by Caterpillar Press for
HarperCollins Publishers Ltd
Suite 2900, Hazelton Lanes
55 Avenue Road
Toronto, Canada M5R 3L2

96 97 98 99   7 6 5 4 3

Canadian Cataloguing in Publication Data
Daigneault, Sylvie
Bruno in the snow
ISBN 0-00-224261-3 (bound)
ISBN 0-00-647953-7 (pbk.)

I. Title.

PS8557.A55B7 1994   jC813'.54   C94-931489-7
PZ7.D35Br 1994

The cold autumn wind had already undressed the
trees in the forest, as the snow, little by little,
covered the leafy ground.

It is in this peaceful forest where Bruno lived
with his parents, Gregory and Clementine.

Clementine had prepared the beds for a long winter sleep and Gregory was already snoring at her side. Soon Clementine was fast asleep, too. But Bruno found himself wide awake.

He stared at the ceiling and listened:

The clock ticked … Tick, tock … Tick, tock.

The mice squeaked … Eek, eek, eek.

Papa snored … Zzzzzzzz.

Bruno slipped out of bed. He grabbed a stool and
stretched up to look out the small window of
the cave. The morning sun was shimmering
on a blanket of fresh white snow.

Bruno was thinking how much fun it would be to
play outside, when he saw his friends, Leo and Leah.
He tapped twice on the window to get their attention.

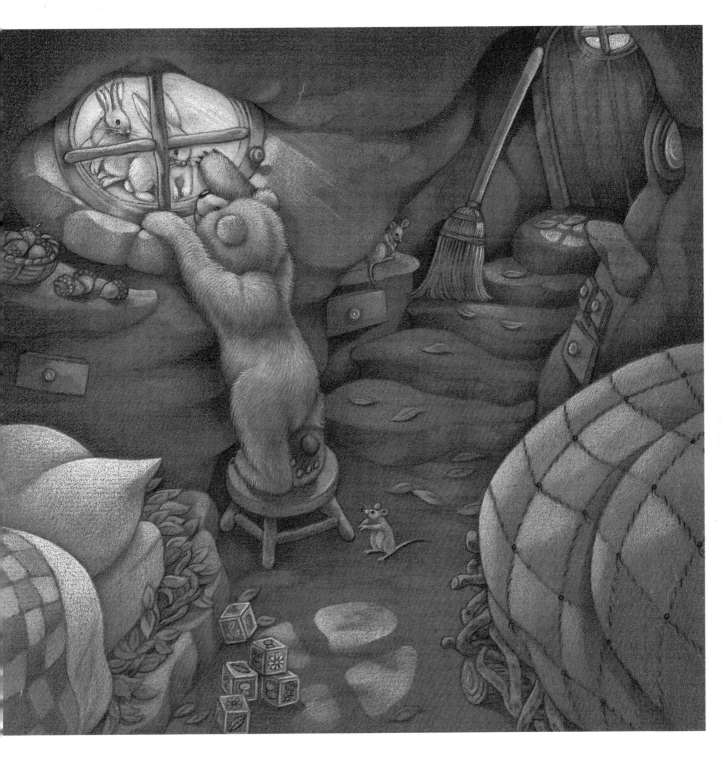

Step by quiet step, Bruno followed the rhythm of Gregory's snoring. He held his breath as he passed the large bed. Then he gently opened the door and snuck away from the cave.

"We're going to visit Edward," said Leo and Leah.
"We'll ride on his sled and borrow his skis.
Come with us!"

Bruno happily followed his friends through the
forest trail. They walked and walked. Bruno's
paws got colder and colder. Soon he could
no longer feel his ears.

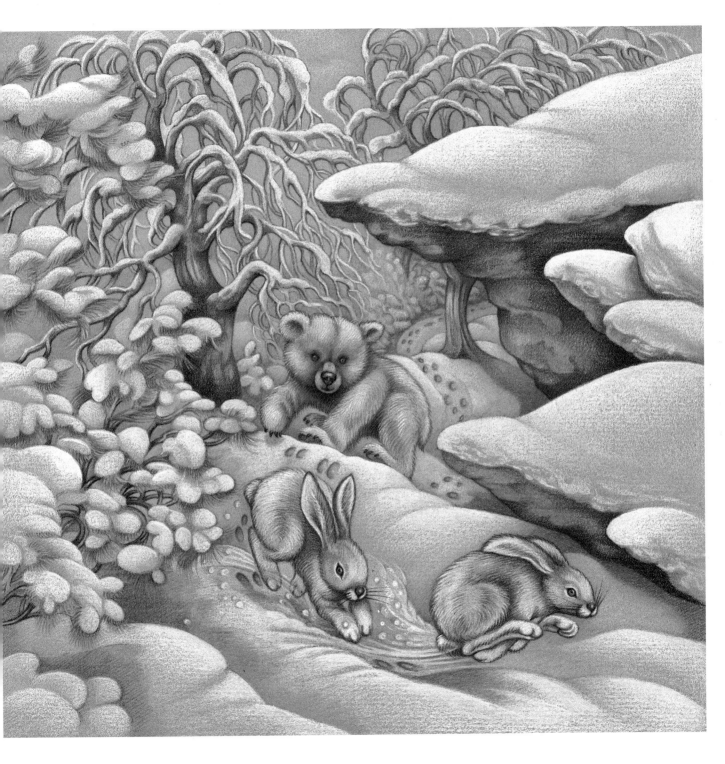

By the time they arrived at the frozen meadows where
Edward lived, Bruno's body felt like ice. He was
glad to sit near the wood stove while Edward
served tea and honey cookies to his guests.

With Edward's help, they learned to apply hot wax on
the skis and sled to get the perfect slide. As they
worked, they listened to Edward's old stories
of the forest. Soon they were all warmed
up and ready to go.

"Good-bye and thank you, Edward," they shouted.

"Now be careful," he replied, "and make sure
you come back before dark."

The three friends eagerly headed
towards the snowy slopes.

The twins gave Bruno his first skiing lesson.

"Bend your knees!" yelled Leo.

"Watch your skis!" shouted Leah.

They both burst out laughing as they watched
Bruno's acrobatics. After sliding, twisting,
bouncing and tumbling on Edward's skis,
Bruno, exhausted, decided to rest on the sled.
Unable to stay awake a moment longer,
Bruno closed his eyes.

Seconds later, Leo and Leah watched helplessly as
the sled headed straight towards the forest.

Through fields and valleys, the sled kept sliding,
taking the sleeping bear right along with it.

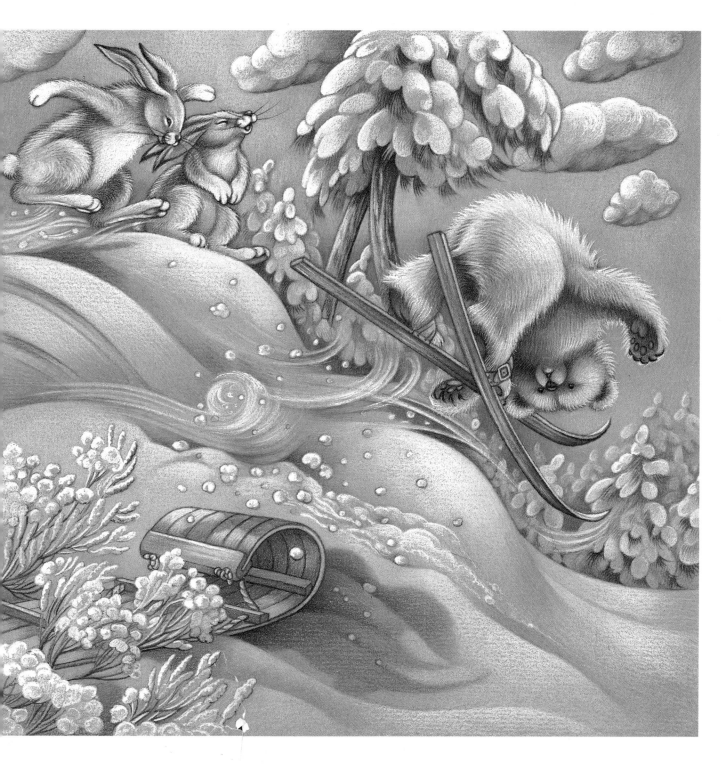

Leo and Leah looked for Bruno everywhere, but
could not find him. Soon the sled tracks had
disappeared under the falling snow,
and they knew they needed help.
They went straight to Edward.

"We have to tell Gregory and Clementine," he said.
"They will be worried sick about Bruno."

After many questions and explanations, Gregory and
Clementine, Edward, Leo and Leah all made their
way through the woods.

There they encountered Alexander, the owl of the forest.
He recalled being disturbed during his nap by a
large object passing by.

Alexander joined the searchers and guided them
towards the village down below.

Meanwhile, in the village, the sled had crashed into
a jumble right in front of Matilda's Toy Shop.

It was Christmas time for the people of the village.
Many brought old and broken toys to Matilda,
who would restore them with love.

When the group of searchers arrived at the village, they saw Matilda bringing a broken sled inside her shop.

Her heart filled with hope, Clementine moved closer. Gregory followed. Suddenly, he gasped. There was Bruno, sound asleep, right in the front window!

Before anybody had time to recover from the shock,
two soft and pudgy hands lifted Bruno and
placed him in the arms of a lady.

The shop was busy and Clementine could not
see Bruno anymore, but her eyes remained
fixed on a large purple hat.

Like spies, they followed the lady home.

The animals crept silently along the walls of the
house. Through the living room window,
they saw the woman placing her gift
under a magnificent Christmas tree.

Then she tucked her little boy into bed
and turned off the lights.

The animals knew about Christmas Eve traditions
and they hurried to put together a clever plan.

Finally, Gregory was ready.

In the middle of the night, the little boy woke up.
He thought he had heard footsteps on the roof.
He looked out the window but all he saw were
the large snowflakes against the moonlight.
His heart pounding, he crept to the top of
the stairs. There was the biggest Santa Claus
he had ever seen, tip-toeing out of the
living room! As quietly as he could,
the little boy scampered back to his room
and jumped into his bed.

On Christmas morning, he was overjoyed to discover
his new teddy bear. Much to her surprise, his
mother found another gift under the tree:
a small jar of honey. The ribbon around it
exactly matched the bow that the teddy bear
was now wearing. "Christmas is certainly
full of magic!" she said.

Back at the cave, Clementine tucked her little Bruno
in his cozy bed and gave him a kiss good-night
that would last until spring.

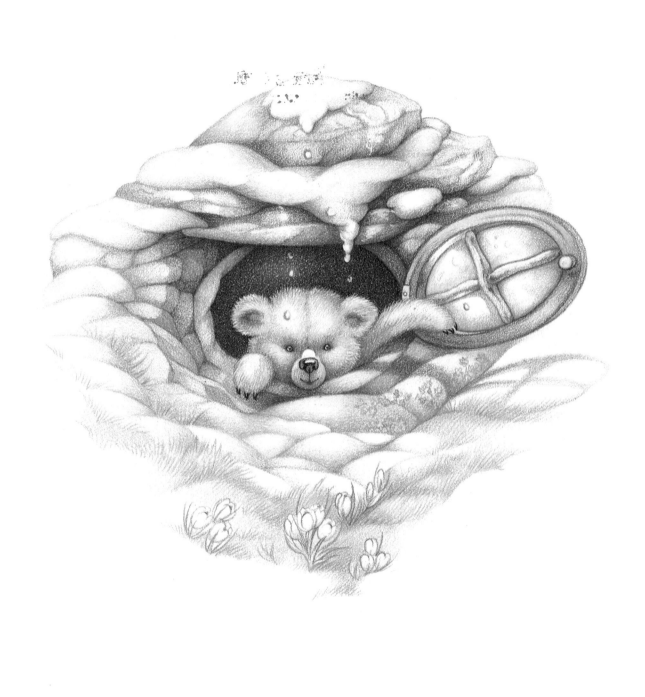